FOR THE TRIXTER,
WHO IS FILLED WITH BIG SURPRISES

Printed in Malaysia

First Edition, September 2017

1 3 5 7 9 10 8 6 4 2

FAC-029191-17160

This book is set in Extravaganza/Fontbros; CG Branding Iron, Girard Slab/Monotype; Adobe Wood Type Ornaments, BadaBoom Pro/Fontspring; Typography of Coop, Fink, Neutraface/House Industries

Library of Congress Cataloging-in-Publication Data

Names: Willems, Mo, author, illustrator.
Title: Sam, the most scaredy-cat kid in the whole world / by Mo Willems.
Description: First edition. • New York : Disney-Hyperion, 2017. • Summary:
   When two fearful children are terrified of each other, their respective
   monsters try to help.
Identifiers: LCCN 2016057932 • ISBN 9781368002141 [hardback] • ISBN 1368002145
   [hardcover]
Subjects: CYAC: Fear—Fiction. Monsters—Fiction. Humorous stories.
   BISAC: JUVENILE FICTION / Social Issues / Friendship. JUVENILE FICTION /
   Monsters. JUVENILE FICTION / Humorous Stories.
Classification: LCC PZ7.W65535 Sam 2017 | DDC [E]—dc23
LC record available at https://lccn.loc.gov/2016057932

Reinforced binding

Visit www.hyperionbooksforchildren.com
and www.pigeonpresents.com

YOUR PAL MO WILLEMS PRESENTS

SAM

the

MOST SCAREDY-CAT KID IN THE WHOLE WORLD

HYPERION BOOKS FOR CHILDREN / NEW YORK

SAM

WAS THE MOST

SCAREDY-CAT

KID

IN THE WHOLE

WORLD.

HE WAS SCARED OF ANYTHING AND EVERYTHING...

ROAR!

ROAR!

ROARY! ROAR!

ROAR!

EXCEPT HIS FRIEND, LEONARDO, THE TERRIBLE MONSTER.

HI, LEO.

ONE DAY,
SAM MADE A
PARTICULARLY
SCARY
DISCOVERY:

FRANKENTHALER AND KERRY.

AAAAAAAAAAAAAAAAAAAAAAH!
AAAAAAAAAAAAAAAAAAAAAH!
AAAAAAAAAAAAAAAAAH!

YELLED SAM.

EEEEEEEEEEEEEEEEEEEEEEEEEEEEEK!
EEEEEEEEEEEEEEEEEEEK!
EEEEEEEEEEEEK!

YELLED KERRY.*

*KERRY WAS THE SECOND-MOST SCAREDY-CAT KID IN THE WHOLE WORLD.

"DON'T WORRY,"
SAID LEONARDO
TO SAM.

"THAT'S JUST
FRANKENTHALER.
SHE'S NICE."

"DON'T WORRY,"
SAID FRANKENTHALER
TO KERRY.

"THAT'S JUST LEONARDO.
HE'S NICE."

"I'M NOT SCARED OF THAT MONSTER!" REPLIED SAM.

"I'M SCARED OF THAT KID!" SAID KERRY.

EEEEEEK!
EEEEEEEEEEK!
EEEEEEEEEEEEEEEEEEEEEK!

YELLED SAM.

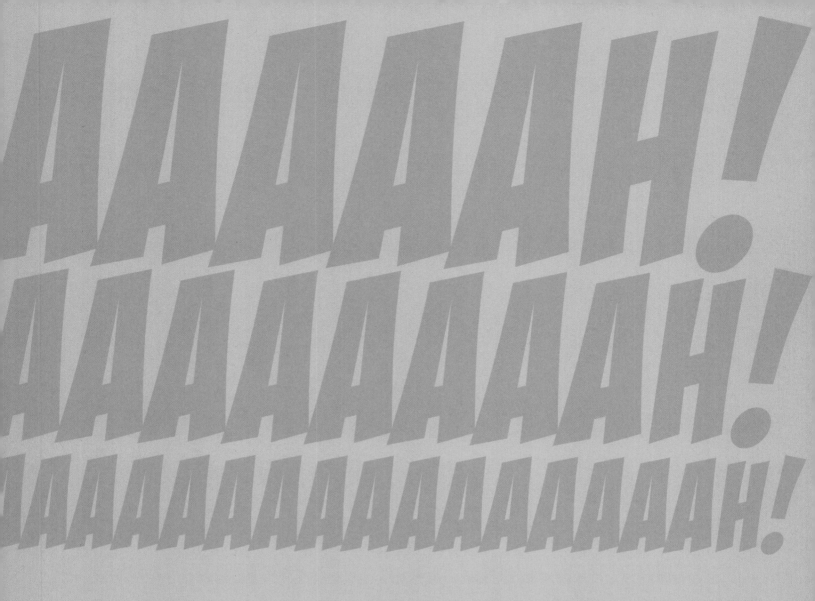

AAAAAH! AAAAAAAH! AAAAAAAAAAAAAAAAAAAAH!

YELLED KERRY.

SOMETHING HAD TO BE DONE.

THEY LEFT.

SAM HAD NO IDEA
WHAT HE SHOULD DO!

KERRY HAD NO IDEA
WHAT SHE SHOULD DO!

SO, THEY HAD
THAT IN COMMON.

TURNS OUT THEY HAD A LOT IN COMMON.

EEEEEEEEEEEEEEEEEEEEEEEEK!

SCURRY-SCURRY-SCURRY-SCURRY-SCURRY-SCURRY-SC

BUT NOT EVERYTHING...

IT WAS CONFUSING

FOR BOTH SCAREDY-CATS.

SO, SAM MADE A **BIG** DECISION

AND SO DID KERRY.

WHEN LEONARDO AND
FRANKENTHALER RETURNED,
THE TWO SCAREDY-CATS
WERE GONE.

TEE-HEE!

SHHHH...

THEY HAD BEEN REPLACED BY TWO NEW FRIENDS.

OF COURSE, LEONARDO AND FRANKENTHALER WERE SURPRISED.

THEY WERE ALSO DELIGHTED.

ROAAARR!!!